This rising moon book belongs to

_____

Way Up in the ARCTIC

Way Up in the ARCTIC

by Jennifer Ward

illustrated by Kenneth J. Spengler

rising moon

Composed in the United States of America
Printed in China

Edited by Theresa Howell
Designed by Sunny H. Yang

The author would like to acknowledge Dr. Kris Hundertmark, University of
Alaska Fairbanks, for his guidance with the facts in the glossary.

FIRST IMPRESSION 2007
ISBN 13: 978-0-87358-928-4
ISBN 10: 0-87358-928-9

07   08   09   10   11   5   4   3   2   1

Library of Congress Cataloging-in-Publication Data

Ward, Jennifer, 1963-
Way up in the Arctic / by Jennifer Ward ; illustrated by Kenneth J. Spengler.
p. cm.
Summary: A counting book in rhyme presents various Arctic animals and their offspring,
from a mother caribou and her little calf one to a mom Arctic fox and her little cubs ten.
Includes related facts.
ISBN-13: 978-0-87358-928-4 (hardcover)
ISBN-10: 0-87358-928-9 (hardcover)
[1. Animals--Arctic regions--Fiction. 2. Animals--Infancy--Fiction.
3. Arctic regions--Fiction. 4. Counting.
5. Stories in rhyme.] I. Spengler, Kenneth, ill. II. Title.
PZ8.3.W2135 Way 2007
[E]--dc22
2006039167

To my nephew. Sam
—J.W.

To my all-grown-up godchildren.
Melanie and Jonathan
—K.S.

Hey, kids!
Look for
the number
hidden on
each page!

Way up in the Arctic in the bright and shiny sun
lived a mother caribou and her little calf **one**.
"Prance!" said the mother. "I prance!" said the one.
so they pranced and they danced in the bright and shiny sun.

Way up in the Arctic near the chilly waters blue
lived a mother polar bear and her little cubs two.
"Nap!" said the mother. "We nap!" said the two.
so they napped and they dozed near the chilly waters blue.

Way up in the Arctic near an ice floe in the sea

lived a pod of white belugas and their little calves **three**.

"Sing!" said the mothers. "We sing!" said the three.

so they sang and they chirped near their ice floe in the sea.

Way up in the Arctic on a cold and icy shore

lived a great herd of walrus and their chubby calves four.

"Wobble!" said the mothers. "We wobble!" said the four.

so they wobbled and they wiggled on their cold and icy shore.

Way up in the Arctic where the moss and lichen thrive
lived a snowy Arctic hare and her little bunnies five.
"Jump!" said the mother. "We jump!" said the five.
so they jumped and they hopped where the moss and lichen thrive.

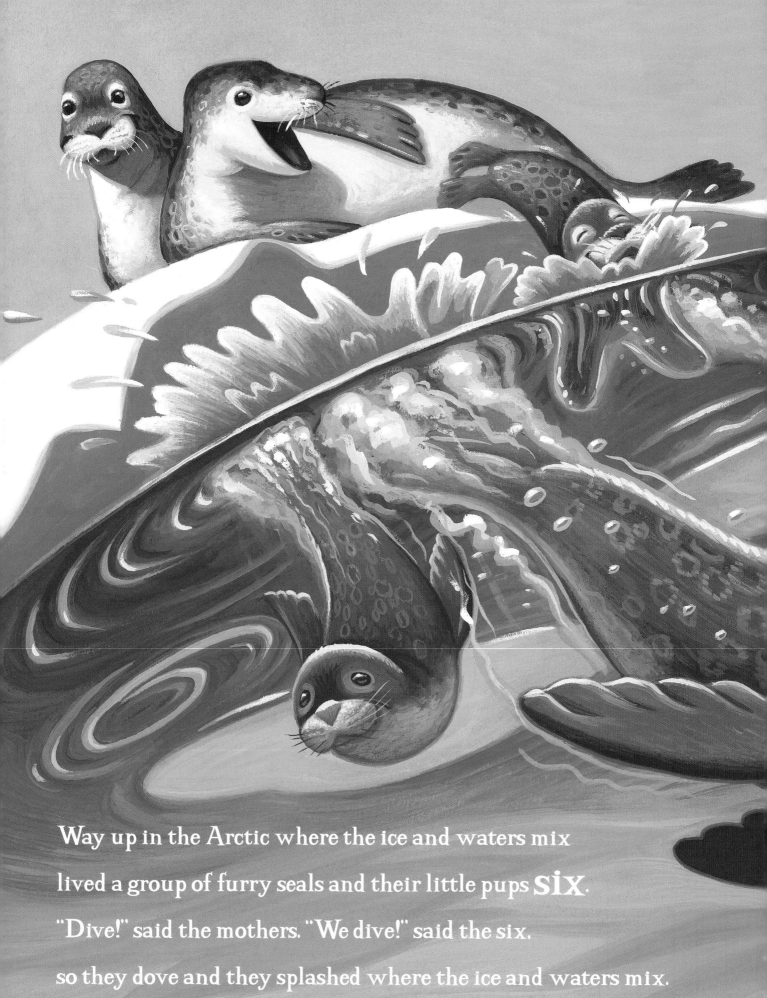

Way up in the Arctic where the ice and waters mix
lived a group of furry seals and their little pups six.
"Dive!" said the mothers. "We dive!" said the six.
so they dove and they splashed where the ice and waters mix.

Way up in the Arctic where the snow falls from heaven

lived a sly mother wolf and her furry pups seven.

"Prowl!" said the mother. "We prowl!" said the seven.

so they prowled and they howled where the snow falls from heaven.

Way up in the Arctic where the sun shines late

lived a mother snowy owl and her little owlets **eight**.

"Hoot!" said the mother. "We hoot!" said the eight,

so they hooted and they snuggled where the sun shines late.

Way up in the Arctic in the snow so fine

lived a quick mother lemming and her wee lemmings **nine**.

"Dig!" said the mother. "We dig!" said the nine.

so they dug and they tunneled through the snow so fine.

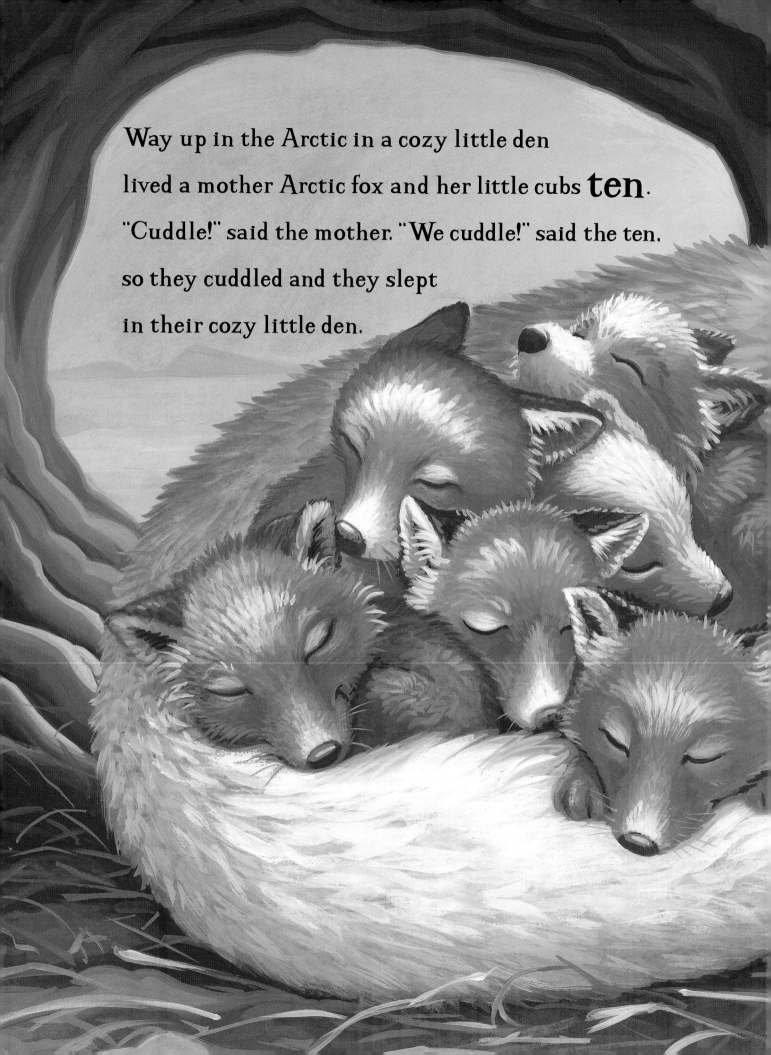

Way up in the Arctic in a cozy little den
lived a mother Arctic fox and her little cubs ten.
"Cuddle!" said the mother. "We cuddle!" said the ten.
so they cuddled and they slept
in their cozy little den.

Cool Facts!

Arctic fox—The Arctic fox is a small fox with short legs and tiny ears. It is also known to have the warmest fur of any land mammal. Like many Arctic animals, the Arctic fox has hair that is white during the winter and brownish during the summer to help it camouflage. Can you think of why an animal would want to be camouflaged?

 Arctic hare—Baby Arctic hares are called leverets. A hare is born with fur and with eyes open. It can also hop around soon after birth. They have large hind feet, which help them to move around on the snow easily—just like giant snow shoes that people wear to help them walk on snow!

Arctic wolf—The Arctic wolf is a large wolf. There's a rule in science called Bergman's Rule. It states that animals within a species that live in a cold climate will be larger than animals of the same species that live in a warm climate farther away. Why? Because the larger the body, the easier it is to keep body heat and stay warm! (Can you imagine how large an elephant species might be if it lived in the Arctic? Would it be larger than African and Asian elephants, or smaller?) The Arctic wolf lives and hunts in social packs. These packs include grown wolf pups that may remain with their parents for several years.

Beluga—Belugas belong to the whale family. They are a toothed whale, and sometimes are called "sea canaries" because of the chatter and noise they make. Belugas are social mammals that live in pods ranging from two to hundreds of whales. When a beluga is born, its skin is grayish in color. As it gets older, its skin turns white. The word "beluga" means "white one" in Russian.

Caribou—Caribou are related to reindeer. They have hollow hair, which helps them to keep warm; the same way wearing a coat in the winter helps keep you warm. Reindeer and caribou are the only deer species where both the male and the female have antlers.

Ice floe—Ice floes are chunks of ice that float and drift in the Arctic Ocean. Many Arctic animals, like the polar bear and walrus, spend much of their time traveling or floating on top of ice floes.

Lemming—A lemming is a small rodent that makes its home in the Arctic. The lemming builds amazing tunnels and burrows through snow! Baby lemmings are born blind, but within two weeks of birth, their eyes open and they begin walking.

Polar bear—The polar bear is the largest meat-eating mammal on the Earth. It is also the largest of all bears. The polar bear is well adapted to living in cold weather. Its skin is black, which helps it to absorb heat from the sun. Like the fur of a caribou, each little hair on its body is hollow like a straw, which helps to trap the heat of its own body and keep the bear warm. Polar bears also have huge feet that help them to swim. A polar bear may have one to three cubs that will stay with their mom for up to two years.

Seal—The Arctic is home to several seal species, and each gives birth to just one pup. All seals are marine mammals, meaning they live in or around water. Certain seal pup species learn how to swim soon after birth, while others stay on ice, nursing and being cared for by their mothers until they are old enough to swim.

Snowy owl—Snowy owls live in the Arctic year round. They are covered with white feathers, which help them blend in with their surroundings. When their eggs hatch, the mother owl stays with the owlets to keep them warm, while the father hunts for food. Unlike most other owls, the snowy owl is a diurnal animal. It is awake by day and sleeps at night.

Tundra—Much of the Arctic is flat and treeless. This area is called the tundra. It is difficult for plants to grow in an area that is so cold and dark for much of the year. The plants that do grow in the Arctic are very special and strong. Many are slow growing mosses and lichen, which can even grow upon rocks.

Walrus—Although it spends most of its time in or near the sea, the walrus is a mammal. It is warm-blooded and has live young, which it nurses. A walrus calf will stay with its mother for two years or more. Both the male and female walrus have tusks, although the tusks on the males are much larger than those found on females. The tusks are two very large, and often long, teeth that come out on either side of their mouth.

Way Up in the ARCTIC

Way up in the Arc-tic in the bright and shi-ny

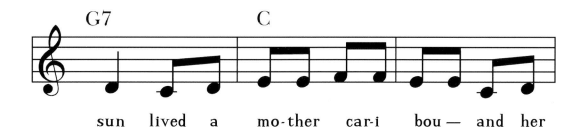

sun lived a mo-ther car-i bou — and her

lit-tle calf — one. "Prance!" said the mo-ther. "I

prance!" said the one. So they pranced and they

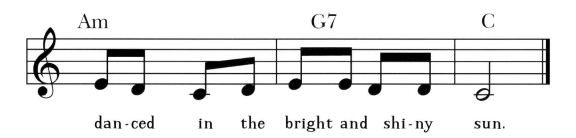

dan-ced in the bright and shi-ny sun.

JENNIFER WARD holds a passion for bringing the wild to life for young readers. She says, "Everyone looks upon Arctic animals with amazement and wonder. As far as places I believe we should protect and hold sacred, it's at the top of my list. It is my hope that children will have fun with this book, and that it will also serve as a springboard of inquiry for them." When not writing from her home in Arizona, she can usually be found prancing through aisles at the public library, tunneling through fiction, digging up facts, and cuddling with a good book by night. Visit her website: www.jenniferwardbooks.com

Photo by Matthew Spengler

KENNETH J. SPENGLER has had a love and closeness with animals for as long as he can remember. As a youth he would play for hours in the woods near his home in Pennsylvania, dreaming he could talk with animals of all kinds. Today, Ken gets to share that enjoyment of nature through the artwork he creates for his many children's books. Some of his titles are *Way Out in the Desert, Kissing Coyotes,* and *Somewhere in the Ocean.* Ken lives in Northern California with his wife, Margaret, and son, Matthew, where they are entertained daily by their two pets, Graycat and Jackie, the circus dog.